For Matthias

A Michael Neugebauer Book · North-South Books / New York / London

LITTLE HOBBIN

By Theodor Storm
Illustrated by Lisbeth Zwerger

Translated from the German by Anthea Bell

Copyright © 1995 by Michael Neugebauer Verlag AG, Gossau Zürich, Switzerland.
First published in Switzerland under the title *Der kleine Häwelmann*
English translation copyright © 1995 by North-South Books Inc.

First published in the United States, Canada, Great Britain, Australia, and New Zealand in 1995
by North-South Books, an imprint of Nord-Süd Verlag AG, Gossau Zürich, Switzerland.

Distributed in the United States by North-South Books Inc., New York.

Library of Congress Cataloging-in-Publication Data is available.
A CIP catalogue record for this book is available from The British Library.
ISBN 1-55858-460-9 (trade binding) 10 9 8 7 6 5 4 3 2 1
ISBN 1-55858-461-7 (library binding) 10 9 8 7 6 5 4 3 2 1
Printed in Italy

My little boy is tired now
and resting on my knee.
As twilight falls, his loving eyes
look tenderly at me.

The time to play is over,
we've put away his toys.
He wants to snuggle close and dream
like all good little boys.

Little Hobbin, dearest, sleep tight;
You fill our home with sunshine bright.
The birds will sing, the children cheer,
When you awake again, my dear.

Once upon a time there was a little boy called Hobbin. He slept in a crib on wheels, but whenever he wasn't tired, his mother had to wheel him around the room in it. Hobbin could never have enough of that, and he wore his poor mother out.

One night little Hobbin was lying in his crib and he couldn't get to sleep. His mother, who was exhausted from wheeling him around all day, had fallen asleep long ago. "Mother!" cried Hobbin. "Wheel me!" So still half asleep, his mother reached out of bed and rolled the crib back and forth, and when her arm felt tired and she stopped to rest, little Hobbin cried: "More, more!" Then she began rolling him all over again.

But finally she fell so fast asleep that she didn't hear him no matter how loudly he shouted. A little later the kind old moon looked in through the windowpanes, and he saw such a funny sight that he rubbed his eyes with the fur cuff of his sleeve in disbelief. There lay little Hobbin in his crib with his eyes wide open, one leg sticking up in the air like the mast of a ship.

He had taken off his nightshirt and hoisted it on his little toe like a sail. Now he took one shirttail in each hand, puffed out his cheeks, and began to blow. And slowly, slowly, his crib began to roll: over the floor, up the wall, upside down along the ceiling, and then down the opposite wall again.

"More, more!" cried Hobbin when he was back on the floor, and he puffed out his cheeks and rolled round the room again, upside down and right side up.

Luckily for little Hobbin, it was night and the earth was standing on its head, or he might easily have broken his neck. When he had made his journey three times, the moon suddenly looked into Hobbin's eyes. "Boy," said the moon, "haven't you had enough yet?"

"No!" cried Hobbin. "More, more!"

"Open the door!" he shouted. "I want to roll through the town.

I want all the people to see me rolling. Open the door!"

"I can't do that," said the kind old moon, but he sent a long

moonbeam through the keyhole, and little Hobbin rolled up

it and out of the house.

It was very quiet and lonely in the street. The tall buildings stood

in bright moonlight, their dark windows staring out blankly.

There were no people to be seen anywhere. As little Hobbin's crib rolled

over the paving stones, making a loud rattling noise, the kind old moon

went with him, shining.

They went up and down the streets, but there were still no people

anywhere in sight.

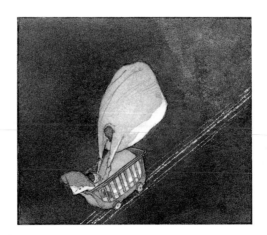

As they were passing the church, the great golden rooster on the steeple crowed for the first time. "What are you doing up there?" little Hobbin called up.

"Crowing for the first time," the golden rooster called down. "The first person will wake up when I crow for the third time."

"I can't wait that long," said Hobbin. "I'm going to roll into the forest. I want all the animals to see me rolling by!"

"Boy, haven't you had enough yet?" said the kind old moon.

"No!" cried Hobbin. "More, more! Shine, old moon, keep shining!"

And with these words Hobbin puffed out his fat cheeks, and the kind old moon kept shining, and they went out of the town gates, across the countryside, and into the dark forest.

It was difficult for the kind moon to get through all the trees.

Sometimes he was left quite far behind, but he always caught up with little Hobbin.

They went uphill and downhill, through fir woods and beech woods. The kind old moon kept shining into all the bushes, but there were no animals to be seen.

There was only a cat, sitting in an oak tree, his eyes glowing in the moonlight.

They stopped. "That's little Tom Cat," said Hobbin.

"I know him. He wants to shine like the stars."

As they went on, the little cat followed. "What are you doing?" little Hobbin called.

"I'm shining!" the little cat called back.

"Where are the other animals?" called little Hobbin.

"Asleep," called the cat. "Can't you hear them snoring?"

"Boy," said the kind old moon, "haven't you had enough yet?"

"No!" cried Hobbin. "More, more! Shine, old moon, keep shining!" Then he puffed out his cheeks, and the kind old moon kept shining. So they went out of the forest and over the moors to the world's end, and straight on into the sky. It was nice up there: All the stars were awake, their wide eyes were twinkling, and the whole sky was shining.

"Watch out!" shouted Hobbin, rolling right into them so that the stars scattered left and right across the sky.

"Boy," said the kind old moon, "haven't you had enough yet?"

And bless me if Hobbin didn't roll right over the kind old moon's nose!

"*I've* had enough!" said the moon, blowing out his lantern. Suddenly all the stars closed their eyes and the whole sky was dark as dark could be.

"More, more!" called Hobbin, but there was no sign of the moon or the stars. They had all gone to bed.

Little Hobbin felt very scared, all alone up in the sky. He took his shirttails in his hands and puffed out his cheeks. He rolled this way and that, back and forth, but he didn't know where he was going and there was no one to see him rolling: no people, no animals, not even the lovely stars.

At last, down below, where the earth met the sky, a round red face looked up at him. Little Hobbin thought the moon had risen again.

"Shine, old moon, keep shining!" he cried. And he puffed out his cheeks and rolled straight across the sky.

But it was the sun rising out of the sea.

"Boy," called the sun, glaring with glowing eyes at Hobbin, "what are you doing here in my sky?"

And with a one, two, three, the sun seized little Hobbin and threw

him into the middle of the sea.

And then what?

Then what? Why, that's when you and I came to the rescue and

picked up little Hobbin in our boat. If we hadn't saved him, he might

well have drowned!